For note makers and note keepers.

Copyright © 2017 by Lizi Boyd.

Library of Congress Cataloging-in-Publication Data:

Names: Boyd, Lizi, 1953– author, illustrator.
Title: I wrote you a note / by Lizi Boyd.
Description: San Francisco, California : Chronicle Books LLC, [2017] | Summary:
Simple text follows the path of a wayward note as each animal, Turtle, Duck, Spider, and many more,
find it and use it for their own purposes.
Identifiers: LCCN 2016026972 | ISBN 9781452159577 (alk. paper)
Subjects: LCSH: Animals—Juvenile fiction. | Letters—Juvenile fiction.
| CYAC: Animals—Fiction. | Letters—Fiction.
Classification: LCC PZ7.B6924 Iar 2017 | DDC 813.54 [E] —dc23
LC record available at https://lccn.loc.gov/2016026972

ISBN 978-1-4521-5957-7

Manufactured in China.

Design by Sara Gillingham Studio.
Hand lettering by Lizi Boyd.
The illustrations in this book were rendered in gouache.

10 9 8 7 6 5 4 3 2 1

Chronicle Books LLC
680 Second Street
San Francisco, California 94107

Chronicle Books—we see things differently.
Become part of our community at www.chroniclekids.com.

I Wrote You A Note

Lizi Boyd

chronicle books · san francisco

I wrote you a note.
Did you find it?

Turtle found
the note.
He made a sail
for his raft.

But the raft went too fast, so Turtle slipped back into the water.

Duck found the note.
She made a dock so her
ducklings could rest.

They ruffled their
wet feathers. Then
they paddled away.

Spider found the note.
He thought it was a bridge.
He crossed the stream.
Eight skinny spider
legs all stayed dry.

I wrote you a note.
Did you find it?

Bird found the note.
She took it to her nest.
Then Bird flew off
to gather grass to
weave the note in.

Squirrel found the note.
He folded it in half
and made a book.
But squirrels don't
sit still for very long.

Squirrel dropped
the book and
scampered up
the tree.

Snail found the note.

She thought it was a house.
Snail said "Hello"
and went inside.
No one was home.

Snail went
inching on her way.

I wrote you a note.
Did you find it?

Mouse found the note.
She made a sun hat.
She worked in her garden
all afternoon.

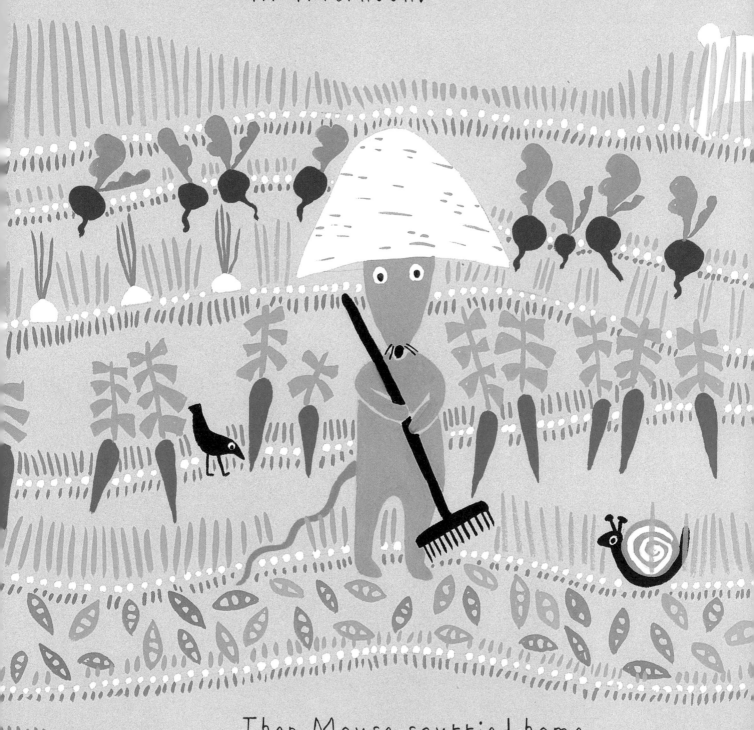

Then Mouse scurried home.

Rabbit found the note.
He made a basket and
filled it with carrots.

Then he ate his lunch
and hurried off,
leaving his basket behind.
Sometimes rabbits are
forgetful.

Dragonfly found the note.
She thought it was a
little napping tent.

When she woke up, she saw Goat.

But Dragonfly was too busy
to talk, so she darted off.

Goat found the note.
"Someone wrote me
a note!" he bleated.
But goats can't read.

Goat went off to graze.

Wind found the note
and tossed it into the sky.

The note twirled

and twisted

then tumbled

down.

I wrote you a note . . .

You found it!

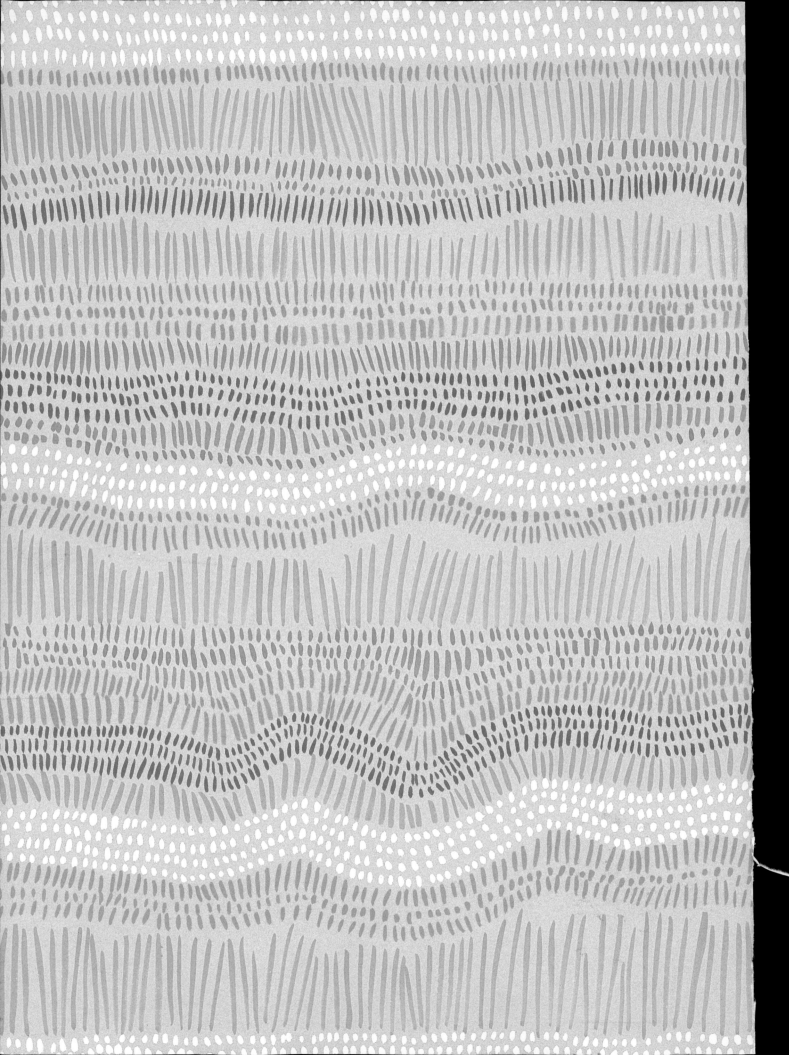